Johnny · Crow's · Garden

LLB.

Johnny Crow's
Party

Tea in the Garden.

OTHER BOOKS WITH
DRAWINGS BY
LESLIE BROOKE ·

JOHNNY CROW'S GARDEN

JOHNNY CROW'S NEW GARDEN

THE GOLDEN GOOSE BOOK
(The Golden Goose   Tom Thumb)
(The 3 Bears   The 3 Little Pigs)

RING O' ROSES
    A Collection of
    Old Nursery Rhymes

THE HOUSE IN THE WOOD
and other Old Fairy Stories

A ROUNDABOUT TURN
    By ROBERT H. CHARLES

THE NURSERY RHYME BOOK
    Edited by   ANDREW LANG

THE TAILOR AND THE CROW

PUBLISHED BY
FREDERICK WARNE & CO

JOHNNY CROW'S PARTY

ANOTHER PICTURE BOOK

DRAWN BY

L·LESLIE BROOKE

LONDON

FREDERICK WARNE AND COMPANY

AND NEW YORK LTD.

FREDERICK WARNE & CO. LTD.
LONDON
ENGLAND

First Edition,	1907
Reprinted	1910
,,	1912
,,	1916
,,	1920
,,	1922
,,	1924
,,	1925
,,	1926
,,	1927
,,	1928
,,	1929
,,	1930
,,	1932
,,	1935
,,	1938
,,	1941
,,	1942
,,	1946
,,	1947
,,	1949
,,	1951
,,	1956
,,	1959
,,	1962
,,	1966
,,	1967

PRINTED IN GREAT BRITAIN FOR THE PUBLISHERS
BY WILLIAM CLOWES AND SONS LTD
LONDON AND BECCLES
190.1066

TO MY NEPHEW
SOMERSET
HAPPY IN A NAME THAT
ASSURES HIS WELCOME
TO JOHNNY CROW'S – OR
ANY OTHER – PARTY

JOHNNY CROW'S PARTY.

Johnny Crow
Plied Rake and Hoe

And improved his little Garden.

And the Eagle

Looked quite regal

In Johnny Crow's Garden.

And the Cockatoo
Said "*Comment vous portez vous?*"

And the Gander

Didn't understand her;

But the Flamingo
Talked the same lingo

In Johnny Crow's Garden.

And the Bear

Sang a sentimental Air,

But the Giraffe
Was inclined to laugh;

Even the Duckling
Couldn't help chuckling
In Johnny Crow's Garden.

Then the Snake

Got entangled with the rake

In Johnny Crow's Garden

And the Cock

Had a very nasty knock;

So the Hen
Said :

"We'll never come again

To Johnny Crow's Garden!"

And the Sheep

Went to sleep,

And the Armadillo

Used him for a pillow;

And the Porcupine

Said: "Wake me if for talk you pine!"

In Johnny Crow's

Garden.

And the Kangaroo

Tried to paint the Roses blue

Till the Camel
Swallowed the Enamel.

And the Reindeer
Said: "I'm sorry for your pain, dear!"

In Johnny Crow's Garden.

So the Chimpanzee
Put the Kettle on for Tea;

And the Seal

Made a very big Meal;

While the Sole
Shared a Muffin with the Mole
In Johnny Crow's Garden.

Then they picked the Flowers, and
wandered in the Maze,
And before they went their several ways

They all joined together
In a Hearty Vote of Praise

Of Johnny Crow and his

Garden.